I0591760

The Confession of Lily Dare

by Charles Busch

FOR PRODUCTION INQUIRIES

UNITED STATES AND CANADA
info@concordtheatricals.com
1-866-979-0447

UNITED KINGDOM AND EUROPE
licensing@concordtheatricals.co.uk
020-7054-7200

Each title is subject to availability from Concord Theatricals Corp., depending upon country of performance. Please be aware that *THE CONFESSION OF LILY DARE* may not be licensed by Concord Theatricals Corp. in your territory. Professional and amateur producers should contact the nearest Concord Theatricals Corp. office or licensing partner to verify availability.

MUSIC AND THIRD-PARTY MATERIALS USE NOTE

IMPORTANT BILLING AND CREDIT REQUIREMENTS

THE CONFESSION OF LILY DARE was originally produced by Theater for the New City Foundation, Inc., Crystal Field, Executive Artistic Director, at Theater for the New City in New York, New York on April 4, 2018. The performance was directed by Carl Andress, with sets and graphic design by B.T. Whitehill, costumes by Rachel Townsend, lights by Kirk Bookman, sound by Bart Fasbender, wigs by Katherine Carr, original song and arrangements by Tom Judson, and Charles Busch's costumes by Jessica Jahn. The production stage manager was Jeffry George. The cast was as follows:

EMMY LOU	Nancy Anderson
MICKEY	Kendal Sparks
AUNT ROSALIE / BARONESS / MRS. CARLTON / LOUISE	Jennifer Van Dyck
LILY DARE	Charles Busch
BLACKIE LAMBERT	Howard McGillin
LOUIS / BARON / DR. CARLTON / MAESTRO GUARDI / PRIEST	Christopher Borg

CHARACTERS

(In Order of Appearance)

Actor 1: **EMMY LOU**

Actor 2: **MICKEY**

Actor 3: **AUNT ROSALIE, BARONESS, MRS. CARLTON & LOUISE**

Actor 4: **LILY DARE**

Actor 5: **BLACKIE LAMBERT**

Actor 6: **LOUIS, BARON, DR. CARLTON, MAESTRO GUARDI & PRIEST**

SETTING

Various locations in San Francisco

TIME

1906 through 1950

LICENSING NOTE

The piano/vocal score for "Pirate Joe" is available through Samuel French, Inc. Please contact your licensing representative for more information.

A NOTE FROM THE PLAYWRIGHT

Over the past forty years, I've written many roles for myself. I've had a dream of a career. I've fantasized, "Wouldn't it be fun to play an ageless vampire actress?" "Wouldn't it be fun to be a temperamental internationally renowned concert pianist?" "Wouldn't it be fun to play a benevolent Mother Superior in a madcap sixties movie?" I've been so fortunate to actually live out those fantasies on stage. My mother died when I was seven and when you lose a parent at a very early age, it marks you forever. All creative writing is personal. You may not even know it, but even the most camp, lightweight theatrical romp derives from some profound place. As an actor / playwright, it's been cathartic creating plays where I can find comfort from a mother or play a loving maternal figure.

In the early 1930s, there was a spate of popular movies later known as the "confession film." The vogue only lasted a few years but all of these gauzy, sentimental movies had remarkably similar plots, in which a young woman gives birth to a child out of wedlock and is forced to give up the baby. Years go by and the mother endures many trials and tribulations: becoming a prostitute, a jewel thief, a bordello madame, and even worse, a cabaret entertainer. Circumstances bring the mother and adult child together and the mother makes her ultimate sacrifice of not allowing her long lost adult child to know her fallen identity. I've always longed to play the mother in one of these stories. It's a tour de force role requiring the actor to go from innocent girl-hood to sophisticated glamorous lady to ravaged decadent outcast. In one evening, you get to be ingénue, leading lady, and character actress. The genesis of *The Confession of Lily Dare* was my desire to go for that challenge.

I work frequently with a wonderful director named Carl Andress. We work closely on a play from the moment I come up with the idea. All of my genre parody plays such as *The Lady in Question*, *Die Mommie Die*, and *The Divine Sister* are stylized comedies but have their dramatic and touching moments. With *The Confession of Lily Dare*, Carl and I wanted to go further and sustain those emotional scenes. Our goal was for the audience to enjoy the outrageous comedy and parodic elements but have the same emotional tug that they would receive if they were watching the original 1930s films. It requires skillful direction and sensitive playing. Our original production had both. We had an excellent cast who could walk that tightrope of parody and sincerity. We never had fun at the expense of the plot. It was absolutely imperative that the audience care about Lily and feel for her plight. There are a number of scenes that establish a comic tone, take a serious turn and then end with a big laugh that releases the tension. An audience has to be guided through that rocky terrain. You want them to laugh when you intend for them to laugh. You want them to lose themselves in the emotion of the story. These plays are a rich stew and it can be so much more rewarding for the cast and audience if you explore all of the textures and flavors. Like the lady of the play's title, I have made the supreme sacrifice of sending my "baby" out into the world. Be gentle with it. Be thoughtful. Appreciate it for all that it aspires to be.

The movies the play evokes are not necessarily great classic films. Some of them aren't easily found. Still, if you are engaged in a production of *The Confession of Lily Dare*, I strongly urge you to do your homework and watch *The Sin of Madelon Claudet*, *Frisco Jenny*, *The Secret of Madame Blanche*, or one or more of the many versions of *Madame X*. Don't expect the audience to be familiar with any of these movies. However, if you are accurate to the tone of them, the audience will appreciate the specificity. They will feel that they are in good hands. It took me awhile in my writing / acting career to realize that I could have my cake and eat it too. I could entertain an audience in a wildly comic way and then surprise them with a moment of true dramatic intensity. Enjoy the ride on the roller coaster. It's exhilarating and enormously satisfying.

– Charles Busch

ACT I

Prologue

(1950, a cemetery outside of San Francisco. **EMMY**, *an aging former prostitute, enters looking for a certain grave and finds it.)*

EMMY. Ahh. Finally! Lil, I've been searching all over for you. Gotta catch my breath. So many different gardens and chapels. And I had to saddle up a trolley, a bus, and a taxi to get myself out here. Lil, I'm sorry it's taken me so long to pay a visit. I have no excuse, other than graveyards give me a huge case of the willies. 'Specially at my advanced years. Any minute I'll be nudging you to move over. Nobody can say this boneyard isn't deluxe. Lil, how in blazes did a sawdust gal get to lie down with the upper crust? And howja finagle the grand tombstone? You should see the stone carving. It's gorgeous...just like you.

*(**MICKEY**, an elderly pianist, enters with a cane.)*

Mickey?

MICKEY. *(Startled.)* Oh!! My heart.

EMMY. Shhh. Calm down. I'm not a **spook.** It's Emmy Lou.

MICKEY. Emmy Lou? What a scare you gave me.

EMMY. The same old Mick. As jumpy as an accountant facing a subpoena. Lordy, it's been ages.

MICKEY. At least a decade. You still married to that fella named Dave?

EMMY. I've been married to three fellas named Dave. You'll have to be more specific. These days I'm a confirmed bachelor girl.

MICKEY. Funny, I never seen you here before.

EMMY. My first, I blush to say. And you?

MICKEY. Oh, I come every week. Rain or shine or rheumatism.

EMMY. No kiddin'? Every week?

MICKEY. I change the flowers. Pick up cigarette butts. And I keep the tombstone clean.

EMMY. The cemetery doesn't take care of it?

MICKEY. All they're good for is some spit on a rag. I use my own mixture of Castile soap, baking soda, powdered chalk, and shh, the secret ingredient...Jack Daniels.

EMMY. Whatever the recipe, that tombstone is as white as a coconut meringue. Between you and me, jitters, how do you figure our girl nabbed herself such a fancy plot?

MICKEY. She was gonna be tossed in an unmarked grave in Potter's Field. Some mystery person stepped in at the last minute to foot the bill. It's the resting place of a great lady.

EMMY. You bet. She was the type of dame who wouldn't let a geezer squeeze her titty for less than a twenty. Didn't she do time in a convent school in Switzerland?

MICKEY. She came straight from the Alpine nuns to live with her Aunt Rosalie in '06. Won't forget that year.

EMMY. Rosalie Mackintosh, the most notorious madame on the Barbary Coast, her only living relative.

MICKEY. Mrs. Mac was a brute but she was fair.

EMMY. As fair as Attila the Hun in an itchy corset.

> (*Lights shift.* **EMMY** *exits.* **MICKEY** *sheds his overcoat, hat and cane. He's now a young man. He sits at the piano.*)

Scene One

(1906, San Francisco. A bordello in the Tenderloin district. **AUNT ROSALIE** *enters. She has the dignified air of a strict governess, which belies what she is: a whorehouse madame.)*

AUNT ROSALIE. Mick, you're doing a lot of sitting at that agony box without playin'. You're not here to daydream.

MICKEY. Mrs. Mac, I ain't daydreamin'. I'm nursing an idea for a classical composition. The Bordello Symphony in four movements: the Madame, the Stoolie, the Flatfoot, the Stooge.

AUNT ROSALIE. How's about a fifth movement? The Nitwit. Now fingers to the keys, Beethoven. And keep your foot soft on the pedal the way I like it.

MICKEY. Sure thing, Mrs. Mackintosh.

*(**MICKEY** begins to lightly play the piano.)*

AUNT ROSALIE. Where is everyone? You'd think it was Palm Sunday. Have you seen Emmy Lou? These newfangled tarts have one customer and then put a "closed for renovation" sign on their privates.

*(**LILY**, an innocent sixteen year old gamine in a pinafore, cape, and broad brimmed hat, enters carrying her small battered suitcase. She's the young Audrey Hepburn and Hayley Mills rolled into one wide-eyed adorable package. She looks around the room bewildered and in awe.)*

Child, you shouldn't be in here. What's the address you're looking for? Speak up.

LILY. 1309 Pacific Avenue. The domicile of Mrs. Rosalie Mackintosh. I must say, it's quite the largest house I've ever seen. A mansion. Golly! That staircase is made of Carrara marble.

AUNT ROSALIE. Kid, you've wandered into a working establishment.

LILY. This *is* 1309 Pacific Avenue?

AUNT ROSALIE. Indeed it is. And I'm Mrs. Mackintosh.

LILY. You are? Well, then, you must be Aunt Rosalie. I'm Lily. Lily Dare. Sarah's child.

AUNT ROSALIE. Sarah's child? I lost track of my sister Sally. Where is she living?

LILY. I wish I could say. I haven't seen Mother in some time. Not since she placed me in a convent school in Bülach, Switzerland. I'm not complaining. It's a fine school. I've learned four languages. *Je parle le francais, ich spreche deutsch, e parlo Italiano, jag pratar flytande Svenska*. Recently, word came in English in the form of a wire that Mother was killed in an avalanche in Tibet. Yours was the name listed as next of kin. There was no money to keep me in the school but the holy sisters were frightfully generous, they really were, and arranged my ship's passage from Europe and the train fare across the country to San Francisco.

AUNT ROSALIE. You're telling me that you travelled all the way here by yourself on ship and train?

LILY. It was an adventure. Chicago was divine, from what I could see from the train. Don't ask me about Topeka. I wrote you several letters. Did you not receive them?

AUNT ROSALIE. The mail ain't as organized in this part of town. I bet before your ma died you didn't even know you had an auntie.

LILY. Oh, I've always known about you.

AUNT ROSALIE. *(Tough and suspicious.)* Whadja hear? And who's talkin'?

LILY. No one in particular. Aunt Rosalie, do you manage some sort of grand hotel? It must be fascinating having

---

* Translation: I speak French, I speak German, I speak Italian, I speak Swedish.

new people coming in and out every day. I love people, especially old grouches.

AUNT ROSALIE. *(Disdainfully.)* You have a cheery disposition.

LILY. I try to find the good in everything and everyone. I make it a game. It's called the happiness game. Shall I teach you how to play it?

AUNT ROSALIE. No. I don't suppose you have a father lurking about.

LILY. Never knew him. Frankly, I don't remember Mother very well. Did she resemble you? You're so very pretty.

AUNT ROSALIE. Sally was a good looking gal and had the gumption to work it. This is what we're gonna do. You can stay here for the present. I'll set up a room for you on the third floor.

LILY. My own room? Really?

AUNT ROSALIE. You'll have a key to the rear entrance on O'Farrell. You're never to be seen coming through the front door or anywhere near these public rooms or the rooms on the second floor. You hear me? If you disobey my orders, I'm not above giving you a good wallop.

LILY. Yes, Aunt Rosalie. If you ever did wallop me, I suppose I would have to tell myself that...

AUNT ROSALIE. *(Interrupting.)* Mickey! Mick is one of the few people on my payroll you can trust. He's a good natured soul, doesn't touch liquor, and won't make any designs on you.

> (**MICKEY** *leaves the piano and crosses over to them.*)

MICKEY. Yes, Mrs. Mackintosh?

AUNT ROSALIE. Mick, this here's my late sister's girl Lily.

MICKEY. Ain't you the cute pixie? And I see an uncanny family resemblance in the vicinity of the schnozzola.

LILY. Funny, because I can't, although I wouldn't mind bearing a...

AUNT ROSALIE. *(Interrupting.)* The child will be boarding here temporarily.

LILY. *(To MICKEY.)* Has anyone ever told you that you could be a double for...

AUNT ROSALIE. *(Interrupting.)* I'm entrusting her in your care. I don't know if we can pull it off but we're gonna try.

MICKEY. Yes, Mrs. Mackintosh.

> (**EMMY** *enters in a bustier, bloomers, and a flimsy kimono.*)

EMMY. Mrs. Mac, I heard you were enquiring after me. I had a little *emergency* on my crushed velvet, if you know what I mean.

AUNT ROSALIE. *Now* you show up. Emmy Lou, you're precisely the type of bad influence I'm seeking to avoid.

EMMY. A bad influence? I'm the only dame you got working here that don't smoke opium or hide a roll of cash in her coozie. *(Warmly.)* Who's this young dear? A new recruit?

MICKEY. Lily. Mrs. Mac's niece.

AUNT ROSALIE. You got a big mouth.

EMMY. *(Genuinely concerned.)* She's not gonna be staying here, is she? This ain't the proper place for a quaint piece as her. Breathing the air would give you the clap.

LILY. The clap? You mean applause?

AUNT ROSALIE. Well, she's gonna be staying here. And don't let me catch you talking to her. Hear me? If by chance you see her up on the third floor, pretend she's a ghost.

EMMY. Yes ma'am. Now if all of you would kindly pardon me, I must put on my Little Bo Peep costume for my two o'clock with the fire chief.

> (**EMMY** *exits but not before giving a warm-hearted wink to* **LILY.**)

AUNT ROSALIE. Lily, I have pressing business. Mickey will take you to your quarters. Mick, it's the room off the attic on the farthest side of the house, where I store my luggage. Set her up with bedding and towels.

MICKEY. I'll be as fastidious as a housemaid at the Saint Francis. Even place a chocolate bon bon on the pillow.

AUNT ROSALIE. Must everyone have a personality? Lily, go along with Mickey. We'll be getting busy soon and the parlor will be filling up.

LILY. Aunt Rosalie... May I... May I kiss you?

AUNT ROSALIE. Kid, if you think you're gonna turn me into a simpering...

>   (**LILY** *kisses her cheek, and in a burst of emotion hugs her tightly.* **ROSALIE** *is suddenly struck with maternal affection. She pulls herself together.*)

Away with you.

>   (**LILY** *starts to leave with* **MICKEY**, *and then turns back.*)

LILY. Aunt Rosalie, I think you're the kindest, dearest, and funniest woman in the entire world!

>   (**MICKEY** *pulls her away.* **AUNT ROSALIE** *is, for once, left speechless. Music plays them off.*)

Scene Two

(1950, back in the cemetery. **MICKEY** *continues his narration.)*

MICKEY. I set her up in that room proper. Filled it with all sorts of pretties. A perfect Valentine of a bedroom for a young lady. Still, it was a lonely life for Lily. Mrs. Mac kept her on the tightest leash. She wasn't allowed to socialize with any of the kids at school. Naturally she couldn't bring anyone home. And the downstairs was strictly off limits. Try enforcing that law.

> *(1906, the front room of the bordello.* **MICKEY** *crosses to the piano.* **LILY** *is singing the last few phrases of a high soprano aria*, accompanied by* **MICKEY** *at the piano.* **EMMY** *watches along with* **LOUIS**, *the handsome young bookkeeper and* **BLACKIE**, *a cynical bon vivant and elegant man-about-town. When she finishes, they all applaud.)*

BLACKIE. Stupendous, my dear. Jenny Lind never sang with such abandon.

EMMY. Honey bunch, you put the nightingales to shame.

MICKEY. Didn't I tell you she was the McCoy?

LOUIS. I see an illustrious future for you, Lily. A dazzling future.

LILY. When Aunt Rosalie hears I have ambitions to be a singer, she'll hit the roof. And she'll go *through* the roof if she catches me down here.

BLACKIE. Don't leave us. It's refreshing to see someone young and full of expectation.

EMMY. I ain't exactly an old hag.

LILY. How does a girl even begin to forge a musical career? It seems hopeless.

---

* A license to produce *The Confession of Lily Dare* does not include a performance license for any third-party or copyrighted recordings. Licensees should create their own.

MICKEY. You gotta keep practicing them scales, biscuit. Day and night.

LOUIS. And reach for the star at the top of the Christmas tree. That also takes practice.

BLACKIE. And it's paramount that you meet the right people. You know one already.

LILY. I do?

EMMY. You're looking at him. Blackie Lambert writes his own ticket in every part of this town from the Tenderloin to Nob Hill.

LILY. But who are you exactly?

BLACKIE. Who am I?

LILY. What do you do?

BLACKIE. What do you think I do?

LILY. I'd take you for a successful novelist or perhaps an architect.

BLACKIE. I'm what is known as a shady character from a once prominent family who adds a veneer of class to whatever room he's in.

LOUIS. Miss Lily, I'm a penniless bookkeeper. A flea-bitten Sir Galahad to be sure, but if I could be of any help to you.

LILY. Louie, you've been more of a help to me than you can ever know. My aunt means well, but there are times I feel like Rapunzel held captive in a tower.

BLACKIE. If Rapunzel had been an acquaintance of mine she would have kept her braid or at least sold it for a hefty profit.

> (**BLACKIE** *seductively attempts to stroke her hair.* **EMMY** *discreetly pulls her away.*)

EMMY. My second husband Pete was the night watchman at the opera house. Kid, I can see you headlining there. Lily Dare in *Il Trovatore*. Ain't that the one where the soprana wears the horns on her head?

LILY. No, Emmy Lou. *Il Trovatore* is an Italian opera by Giuseppe Verdi. Brünnhilde is a character in three of Wagner's operas: *Siegfried, Die Walküre,* and *Götterdämmerung.* Of course, I've never actually been to the opera.

MICKEY. It ain't cheap. We could try sneaking into the second act?

LOUIS. She has to see the performance from the beginning. One can get standing room for next to nothing. I'm in possession of a tuxedo with a few well-situated moth holes. May I be your escort?

LILY. Louie, I can't think of anything more sublime.

BLACKIE. Dear boy, our Lily's introduction to the San Francisco Opera must not be in standing room, but in my box in the dress circle. You will be my guest.

(**AUNT ROSALIE** *enters.*)

AUNT ROSALIE. Lily! What are you doing down here? Emmy, I've warned you. Mickey, I thought you knew better. Louie, I could fire you for this.

EMMY. Pardon me for interruptin'. It's twenty minutes to the hour and I must put on my nanny costume for my five o'clock with the comptroller.

(**EMMY** *exits.*)

BLACKIE. Madame Rosalie, you left me out of your tirade*.

AUNT ROSALIE. Blackie, I'm trying to exert some discipline. You're not helping.

LILY. Aunt Rosalie, it's my fault. I came from my singing lesson and was showing off my new aria.

AUNT ROSALIE. Down here? That's a fine move, young lady, singing in a bawdy house. I catch you again and I'll stop paying for them singing lessons.

LOUIS. Mrs. Mackintosh, your intentions are admirable but Lily might as well be locked up on Alcatraz.

AUNT ROSALIE. The day hasn't dawned when I take advice from a dime a dozen bookkeeper.

---

* Pronounced, as the French: Tee-rod.

LOUIS. Even a lowly bookkeeper has eyes and ears and a heart.

AUNT ROSALIE. Don't think I don't know you were seen with Lily in the park and by the wharf. I've got spies in every quarter of this town.

LILY. Aunt Rosalie, you mustn't speak to Louie that way. He's my friend.

LOUIS. She needs a friend.

AUNT ROSALIE. Louie, you're fired. I don't ever wanna see you on these premises again.

LILY. Aunt Rosalie!

AUNT ROSALIE. You try and see my niece on the sly, I'll fix you but good. Now get out of here! You heard me. Get out of here!

LOUIS. Lily, you know where to find me.

(**LOUIS** *exits.*)

LILY. You can't fire Louie. You can't.

AUNT ROSALIE. I can and I did. Go to your room.

LILY. *Vous êtes un harridan deraisonnable**!

(**LILY** *runs from the room.*)

AUNT ROSALIE. How dare she talk to me in that crude manner? Wha'd she say?

BLACKIE. My dear Madame Rosalie, you seem to have lit the flames of defiance. Viva la Lily.

AUNT ROSALIE. The nerve of that kid. The little ingrate needs a well-deserved swat on her Puccini.

(*She slaps her own behind for emphasis.*)

---

* Translation: You are an unreasonable harridan!

Scene Three

(1906, the front room of the bordello. **LILY** *and* **LOUIS** *embrace.)*

LOUIS. When will your aunt be returning?

LILY. Not till tomorrow. It's perfectly wicked that you should be forced to sneak into this house, when utter strangers perform sexual intercourse in our parlor. Please, Louie, take me away from Pacific Avenue. Can't we run off and be married? I don't need to finish school.

LOUIS. How proud I would be to have you as the bearer of my name and mother to my children. I see you stout as a partridge, parading through Huntington Park; Mrs. Louis Markham and her brood of twelve. As it is, I'm barely able to support myself, my fragile hummingbird.

LILY. Fragile? I survived steerage, a train ride across the desert, and an hour in Topeka.

*(**AUNT ROSALIE** enters from the front door.)*

AUNT ROSALIE. Well, ain't this a pretty pass.

LILY. Aunt Rosalie, you were supposed to be in Seattle at a whorehouse convention.

AUNT ROSALIE. A birdie told me to come back early. And here I thought you were good. I thought you were decent. Now I see that you're made of the same dirt as your mother and me.

LOUIE. She is good! As virtuous a girl as there ever was. Mrs. Mackintosh, we're going to be married.

AUNT ROSALIE. Over my dead body you'll marry this child.

(A loud rumbling is heard.)

What's that rumble?

LILY. Everything is shaking.

LOUIS. It's an earthquake! Lily!

(Sounds of destruction are heard. Imaginative special effects. Blackout.)

Scene Four

(A hill just out of the city. **MICKEY** *and* **EMMY** *are drinking soup out of tin mugs.)*

MICKEY. Well, I've had my fill of sleeping under the stars. Some refugee camp. There's a rock permanently installed in my lower lumbar region.

EMMY. Never did I reckon I'd be back to drinking soup made of grass.

MICKEY. It could be worse. You could be buried underneath the grass.

EMMY. You're a great comfort, Mickey dear.

MICKEY. I keep thinking there's gonna be another quake. My nerves are a frazzle under the best of circumstances. Comes from growing up next door to a firecracker emporium. Should we hoof it and continue searching for people we know?

EMMY. One special young person? That part of town was hit the worst. What wasn't toppled over was destroyed by fire.

MICKEY. I feel in my soul that our girl is alive. Lily's tough. She's a survivor.

EMMY. Well, then we won't give up. Will we? Whew. Ten days without a bath. I'm smelling like a plate of short ribs that's been left too long on the steam table. I don't know how you can bear being with me.

MICKEY. To be frank, it's not easy.

EMMY. To be frank, you're not smelling like a field of lilacs either. Mickey! Look! Is that who I think it is? It is? It's Lily. She's alive!

MICKEY. I knew she'd get through this! Lily! Lily! Over here!

*(**LILY** stumbles on.)*

LILY. Emmy! Mickey!

MICKEY. I told Emmy you were of stern stuff.

(The three of them embrace.)

EMMY. It's a fifty dollar miracle is what it is.

LILY. Didn't think I'd ever see either of you again. I've trudged from one refugee camp to another. I'm so tired. So hungry.

*(**MICKEY** hands her his cup of soup.)*

MICKEY. Here, sip this. And don't ask what's in it.

*(**LILY** sips the soup.)*

LILY. Mmm. It's as good as anything off the table of Le Cordon Bleu.

EMMY. The house? It's destroyed?

LILY. Came down around our heads. I don't know how I wasn't killed. Everyone else. All the girls. Pearl, Magda, Lizzie. Crushed. Aunt Rosalie. Decapitated.

MICKEY. And Louie? He was with you that day.

LILY. Crushed and decapitated. To the very end, he tried to protect me. Oh, Mick, Emmy Lou, he never knew this. I'm going to have his baby.

Scene Five

*(1950, **MICKEY** at the cemetery.)*

MICKEY. Somehow or other, we got by. There's always work to be found for a piano player who knows ragtime and a hooker who does anal. The three of us were able to commandeer a roof over our heads in a hovel in Chinatown. Soon there were four of us.

(1906, a room in Chinatown.)

*(**LILY** lies on a cot in deep despair. **EMMY** holds the swaddled newborn baby in her arms. **MICKEY** looks on, exhausted from a job well done.)*

EMMY. Aw, isn't she the cutest dickens? The cutest dickens.

MICKEY. We brought her into this world but good. That birth was the work of professionals. And with no rehearsal.

EMMY. She showed up in twenty minutes flat, as if she was racing to catch the last trolley.

LILY. You brought her into a foul, ugly world.

MICKEY. We'll get by. We'll have to.

EMMY. I bet if you held the snookums, the future wouldn't seem so bleak.

LILY. I don't want it. I don't want it.

MICKEY. You mustn't talk that way.

EMMY. Take a look at her. She's already got a golden curl. On the road to being a famous beauty. Come on. Take a peak.

LILY. I prayed it would die.

EMMY. Not the baby, Lily.

LILY. I wish it was dead. I wish we were both dead. Why didn't I die with Louie? Louie!

MICKEY. She's a piece of him, Lily. She's a living piece of him.

(**EMMY** *places the baby in* **LILY**'s *arms.*)

LILY. Oh no, take it away. Take it away.

(*Emotional music builds.* **LILY** *stares at the baby, at first in bitterness. Gradually her maternal instinct takes over and she gazes at the baby with serene adoration.*)

She does look a bit like him. Doesn't she? We shall call her Louise.

Scene Six

(1950. **EMMY** *continues her narration.)*

EMMY. Once she got used to the notion, Lily could have been voted mother of the year. Oh, the way she doted on that infant. It became clear that if the baby was to be properly taken care of, we were gonna need cash and plenty of it. Who in the new San Francisco had that kind of dough? I'll tell you who. The same bloodsuckers that squeezed every drop out of the old San Francisco. Our girl was desperate. Yep, it was plain old fashioned sweaty palmed desperation that brought her to visit Mr. Blackie Lambert in his plush new digs on Nob Hill. I don't know how that snake did it but he managed to slither out of the earthquake's rubble with a cool profit.

(1906, **BLACKIE**'s *luxurious apartment.)*

*(***LILY*** *visits* **BLACKIE**, *who is garbed in an elegant silk dressing gown. She affects a vivacious manner in order to get what she wants.)*

BLACKIE. Lily Dare. What a welcome surprise.

LILY. My profuse apologies.

BLACKIE. Why apologize?

LILY. I was not brought up to pay calls on friends unannounced. Mother Angelica in the convent would have been appalled at my gaucherie.

BLACKIE. Well, then we shall keep this a dark forbidden secret from sainted Mother Angelica.

LILY. Blackie, I've missed you so. I've always looked upon you as a sort of a magical Uncle Drosselmeyer in *The Nutcracker.*

BLACKIE. And you have been most appreciative of whatever token I've given you.

LILY. It would be unattractive to accept anything else.

BLACKIE. Not even a jeweled Fabergé egg?

LILY. Well, a small one. To be polite.

BLACKIE. Lily, you're incorrigible and irresistible. When one hasn't seen an old friend the assumption is that they died in that inopportune disaster.

LILY. You've risen from the ashes alive and with your style of living improved.

BLACKIE. It's a talent, my dear, and a flair for seizing the opportunity when it presents itself. Lily, how rewarding to see that the outrageous child has blossomed into beautiful womanhood. And topped by such a *cunning* chapeau.

LILY. You would notice that, you devil. One of my aunt's girls has taken up millinery in her retirement. I'm doing her a favor by wearing one of her hideous creations. Is it quite pathetic?

BLACKIE. Yes, but you sport it with panache. I heard of your aunt's untimely death. Did she leave you a healthy bequest?

LILY. Not so much that one could erect a new City Hall but enough for fun and frolic. The trouble is that everyone is so tediously busy rebuilding. There's no one to laugh with and be devil-may-care.

BLACKIE. Your young life doesn't appear all that grim. I caught a glimpse of you last week at the opening night of Maude Bentley in *Comtesse Maxine*. At least I fancy it was you.

LILY. Oh, that was me. I worship Maude Bentley. She's by far the best dressed woman on the American stage.

BLACKIE. And it marked the first night of the newly restored Majestic Theater. What did you think of the magnificent fresco of the nine muses above our heads?

LILY. Heavenly. The entire evening was celestial.

BLACKIE. A pity there isn't a tenth muse for liars.

LILY. I beg your pardon?

BLACKIE. You weren't there that night. That was a falsehood.

LILY. But I was. Must I present with you with the souvenir program?

BLACKIE. That would prove difficult given the fact that *Comtesse Maxine* was not playing at the Majestic.

LILY. It wasn't? Well, I've been to the theatre so often these past few weeks, I-I-I suppose I've...

BLACKIE. The Majestic Theatre no longer exists except as a neglected pile of brick and plaster. Furthermore, there is no play with the title *Comtesse Maxine.*

LILY. I was there to see Maude Bentley. The flimsy vehicle was of little or no concern to me.

BLACKIE. How loyal, except for one detail. There is no such actress as Maude Bentley! There is an Irene Bentley and a Maude Adams, but no Maude Bentley! I invented her to trick you. That you fell for it is an insult to all aging actresses and the sodomites who love them.

LILY. I can explain! I-I-I...

BLACKIE. It was a stupid lie. Easy to expose. Unworthy of you. And here I thought you had stopped by with a nostalgic yen to go over old times.

LILY. Oh, but I did. You must believe me. I-I-I...

BLACKIE. I believe you are one of the many dreary unfortunates left behind in the debris*. You have come here, my dear Lily, for a handout.

LILY. A spurious and uncouth accusation.

(**BLACKIE** *grabs her arm.*)

BLACKIE. Out with it!

LILY. Let me go! You're hurting me!

BLACKIE. No more lies! No more evasions!

(**BLACKIE** *lets go of her arm.*)

LILY. Yes, Blackie. I *am* one of those "unfortunates" you speak of with such contempt. I'm penniless. Half starving.

---

* Pronunciation: DEB-ree.

BLACKIE. As I imagined.

LILY. It's quite beyond your imagination. Things couldn't be worse. We're down in Chinatown barely existing in a dark airless tenement. Rats and cockroaches dance a gavotte in our shoes. The thin mattress I sleep on reeks of five generations of urine stains.

BLACKIE. You paint a vivid picture.

LILY. At the street level, there's a chop suey den. A twelve year old busboy named Tso occasionally manages to steal for us some chicken cartilage and drowns it in their house special sauce. For his daring, I've nicknamed him General Tso. This is how we live, but I refuse to bow down in defeat.

BLACKIE. A sterling attitude. I commend you for it. However, bravery, as with French poetry, bores me.

LILY. I have come to you for help. You're my last resort. You see, I have a baby now. A little girl named Louise.

BLACKIE. Ahh. And in the tradition of the women in your family, I presume the bastard child has no father?

LILY. Her father was my aunt's bookkeeper, Louis Markham.

BLACKIE. Ah, yes, Louis. A young man profoundly afflicted with sincerity.

LILY. We were to be married but he was killed in the earthquake. I'll do anything to keep my baby clothed and fed. I thought an operatic career could be the answer. And you know everyone.

BLACKIE. Success as a coloratura is an ambitious proposition. There are *other* forms of lighter entertainment that can yield immediate reward. Turn around. With that face and that voice and that figure, I might be able to do *something* with you.

LILY. What exactly have you in mind?

BLACKIE. From the first, I perceived a *soupçon* of mystery behind your school girl insouciance. That is a quality we can exploit. We are an unlikely Pygmalion and Galatea, you and I. But why not? Within a year, my pet, I will transform you into the most glittering sought after cabaret entertainer in San Francisco, New York, London, and Paris. What do you say to that?

LILY. San Francisco will be sufficient, thank you.

BLACKIE. Our next lesson. Never settle for a mere oyster in the sand, Lily. The sea is full of riches. One might discover a sunken ship overflowing with gold and jewels.

LILY. I suppose the charitable word to describe you would be "pirate."

BLACKIE. I can very well see myself steering my ship off the coast of Mandalay. *(Pondering.)* Mandalay. That would make rather a good name for an alluring cabaret entertainer.

LILY. Just Mandalay?

BLACKIE. That is all you need...besides me.

(**BLACKIE** *spins her around and they both dissolve in laughter as the lilt of a waltz swells.)*

Scene Seven

(1909, a fashionable cabaret, the Chateau le Noir, San Francisco.)

(A decadent Austrian **BARON** *and* **BARONESS** *have been seated at a ringside table.* **MICKEY** *enters in his smart tuxedo. The* **BARON** *gestures for him to come to their table.)*

MICKEY. Were you waving to me, sir?

BARON. Waiter, is this table the closest to the stage? My wife, the baroness, and I have journeyed from Austria to see the fabled Mandalay.

MICKEY. Oh, I'm not the waiter or the maître d'. I'm Miss Mandalay's musical accompanist.

BARON. An unconscionable faux pas. I should have known by your hands. The pale unearthly fingers of an artist.

BARONESS. *(Intrigued.)* Curiously feminine*.

MICKEY. Baron, I can vouch that here at the Chateau le Noir the tables are carefully arranged so every paying customer can give Mandalay the once over. Helps that she's got a mug with no bad angles.

BARON. And you, sir, possess the rosy plump cheeks of a corrupt choirboy. How long have you have you been performing with la Mandalay? *(With sudden ferocity.)* How long?

MICKEY. Me and her go way back.

BARONESS. It is whispered that she was born in the streets of Sumatra, weaned by a king cobra, and raised among circus folk in Constantinople.

MICKEY. That sounds about right.

*(**BLACKIE** enters in his black tie and tails and approaches the **BARON** and **BARONESS**.)*

---

* Pronunciation: Femi-neen.

MICKEY. Now if you will excuse me, your, um, nobilities, la Mandalay requires my singular attention in her dressing room boudoir.

(**MICKEY** *self-consciously bows and speedily exits.*)

BLACKIE. Baron, I welcome you and the baroness to the Chateau le Noir. I am Blackie Lambert, *le proprietaire du cabaret** and your host.

BARON. The room has great elegance. One is reminded of the cabarets of Budapest and Monte Carlo.

BLACKIE. I know them well. My family, though not of titled lineage, roamed the world in bankrupt yet luxurious exile.

(*Indicating the third seat.*)

May I?

BARON. *Es wäre uns eine freude, Herr Lambert***.

(**BLACKIE** *sits with them.*)

BLACKIE. Baron, you are clearly a gentleman of travel. This cannot be your first visit to San Francisco.

BARON. Shockingly so. The Baroness Leda and I have been told your city is the Dubrovnik of the United States.

BARONESS. (*Groaning.*) Tell me it is not as charmingly *picturesque* as Dubrovnik.

BLACKIE. You will find, baroness, that there is a San Francisco...and then, there is a...San Francisco.

BARONESS. (*Darkly.*) This *other* San Francisco whets my appetite. (*With strange intensity.*) In fact, I demand a midnight tour.

BLACKIE. My adventurous baroness, that can be arranged.

BARON. Your enigmatic star, Mademoiselle Mandalay, is the stuff of legend.

---

* Translation: Proprietor of the cabaret.

** Translation: It would be our pleasure, Mr. Lambert.

BLACKIE. The lady has captured the imagination of our citizenry as few have.

BARONESS. One hears much and yet so little.

BLACKIE. Mandalay is an artist of supreme sophistication, who can be as stubbornly opaque as a milkmaid.

BARON. A milkmaid, *ja*, squeezing ever tighter the cow's um *(Struggling for the word.) sitze.*

BARONESS. The cow's teat, *mein liebling**. Her teat.

BLACKIE. The capricious Mandalay derives the same euphoria from a Bach fugue as she does peering for hours at a grasshopper.

BARON. A creature pinned into submission with a well-placed needle. Mr. Lambert, to merely hear her sing would be a torment. Will the baroness and I have a chance to speak with her? Alone?

BLACKIE. Mademoiselle is a mystery that rather enjoys being...

BARON. Investigated?

BLACKIE. Explored. Alas, she is a mystery doomed to remain unsolved. Then, that is part of her tragic allure.

BARONESS. You are making my husband drool. His spittle is unbecoming.

BLACKIE. Baron, a private audience is not beyond the realm of possibility. *Mais naturellement***, for this invasion of her cherished solitude, the lady is not averse to accepting a well-chosen gift. My honored guests, I must put an end to the brutal suspense and relinquish my star to her ravenous public.

(**BLACKIE** *bows and leaves the* **BARON** *and* **BARONESS.** *He steps onto the stage.*)

Dear friends and fellow sybarites, the Chateau le Noir aims to provide this fabled hamlet of debauched revelry with entertainment that ranges from the ribald

---

* Translation: My darling.
** Translation: But naturally.

to the exquisite. Tonight, I give you that Titian-tressed empress of melody, the ruby-maned Delilah of the El Camino Real, whose throaty warbling would arouse Samson to make an appointment for a permanent wave. The scintillating, the glamorous, the elusive Mandalay.

> (**LILY** *enters bejeweled and gowned, evoking Marlene Dietrich. Accompanied on the piano by* **MICKEY**, *she sings a torch song.*)

[MUSIC "PIRATE JOE"]

LILY.

MEN HAVE SAILED 'ROUND THE GLOBE
IN SEARCH OF TREASURE
IN SEARCH OF PLEASURE
I'VE KNOWN QUITE A FEW OF THEM
I LOVE THEM THEN I'M THROUGH WITH THEM

THEY'RE TOO COARSE
THEY'RE TOO ROUGH
THEY'RE JUST LOSERS
BUT I KNOW ONE WANDERING SEAMAN
HE'S NOT A BRUTE
HE'S NOT A "HE-MAN"
AND HE CAN LAY DOWN HIS ANCHOR
FOR AS LONG AS HE CHOOSES

BUT I'LL NEVER BE THIS SAILOR'S BRIDE
AS LONG AS HE'S OFF WITH THE TIDE

PIRATE JOE
WHY HAVE YOU GONE AWAY?
PIRATE JOE
WHAT DO YOU SEEK THE MOST?
WON'T YOU EVER STOP SEARCHING FOR GOLD?
DON'T YOU KNOW THAT A JEW'L YOU CAN HOLD
IS WAITING HERE?
ON THE BARBARY COAST

(To an audience member.) Hey, mister, why the sad face?

NOW, PLEASE DON'T YOU THINK
THAT WHILE JOE'S OUT ON THE DRINK
I'M SAD AND LONELY
(DEAR GOD, IF ONLY!)

I'M CONSTANTLY SURROUNDED
I'M COURTED AND I'M HOUNDED
BY WEAKLINGS WHO ARE GLAD TO BE MY SLAVES
BUT IT'S NOT FUN BEING A SIREN
TO A SIDNEY OR A MYRON
WHEN THE MAN THAT *I'M* IN CHAINS FOR
IS RIDING O'ER THE WAVES
PIRATE JOE
WHY HAVE YOU GONE AWAY?
PIRATE JOE
WHAT DO YOU SEEK THE MOST?

WON'T YOU EVER STOP SEARCHING FOR GOLD?
DON'T YOU KNOW THAT A JEW'L YOU CAN HOLD
IS WAITING HERE
ON THE BARBARY COAST

> (**LILY** *takes a break between verses. She is
> approached by the* **BARON**.)

BARON. *Mein gnadiges fraulein*, your performance has
been a revelation. I am the Baron Kinsky von Esterhazy-
Trauttmansdorff-Cavriani-Graetz. My intimates call
me Zou Zou.

LILY. Mmm. I like that name. It does good things for the
face. Zou Zou.

BARON. Do that again. I implore you.

LILY. I'd rather not.

BARON. I shall bestow on you the Trauttmansdorff emerald.

LILY. Zou Zou.

BARON. Repeat my name and I'll give you the Cavriani
sapphire.

LILY. Zou Zou. And here's one on the house: Zou.

---

* Translation: My gracious lady.

BARON. Would you join us at our table? My wife, the Baroness Leda, must savor this unique experience.

LILY. I don't usually meet the wives...except in court.

BARON. Shall we?

(The **BARON** *leads* **LILY** *over to the table.)*

My darling, la Mandalay has consented to join us.

BARONESS. Ah, mademoiselle, you are even more beautiful away from the stage.

LILY. I thank you, baroness.

BARON. What resplendent diamond earrings. May I ask the impertinent question of how you came to acquire this adornment?

LILY. You *are* impertinent, Herr Baron. The earrings were a gift from an admirer.

BARON. I know the value of such stones. I'd say his admiration was considerable.

LILY. Herr Baron, you show an interest in women's jewelry. Are you a transvestite?

BARONESS. You are indeed insightful, mademoiselle. My husband has an erotic mania for women's fashion accessories.

LILY. Good to know. I'll keep him away from my ear muffs.

BARON. Heartless.

BARONESS. My husband is an ardent collector of the mythological and the zoological.

BARON. And the gynecological. I am also a sculptor. Ah, to take a chisel and carve a life sized nude statue of you. It shall be composed of flesh colored beeswax and human hair and be anatomically correct in its every detail.

LILY. And still you would never know me.

BARONESS. Mademoiselle Mandalay, I accept the challenge of plumbing your cavernous depths. I have a small laboratory at our castle in Kreuzenstein.

LILY. Um... Where is this going?

BARONESS. It is the inner sanctum from where I concoct my own perfumes. Before you ascend the modeling stand, I would bathe you in a fragrance created for you and about you.

LILY. Mmm. A hint of lavender. Herr Baron, baroness, I have yet to finish my first number. I may have missed the key change.

> (**LILY** *returns to the spotlight to finish her song.*)

AT DAYBREAK I CAN SCAN THE HORIZON
IT'S MY DESTINY THAT I'VE GOT MY EYES ON
WHAT SWEET FUTURE THE CURRENT WILL BRING
AND THEN THIS IS THE SONG I WILL SING:

PIRATE JOE
NOW YOU'VE COME BACK TO ME!
PIRATE JOE
I'M WHAT YOU SEEK THE MOST!
I DON'T CARE 'BOUT YOUR SILVER AND GOLD
'CAUSE I'VE GOT ME A GUY I CAN HOLD
HE'S SO MANLY, SO VIRILE, SO BOLD!
AND HE'LL STAY WITH ME
HERE ON THE BARBARY COAST!

> (*Applause. The* **BARON** *and* **BARONESS** *have left their table.* **BLACKIE** *takes her by the arm and pulls her to the side.*)

BLACKIE. Lily, I must talk to you immediately. Come with me to the office.

LILY. What's wrong? Something has happened.

BLACKIE. The police are outside the club.

LILY. Why should the police be here?

BLACKIE. Those earrings you're wearing. They're stolen.

LILY. Stolen? It was your sentimental gesture upon signing our contract.

BLACKIE. I was under the impression they were on loan from the jeweler. He claims otherwise. The state prosecutor has waited over a decade to pin something on me. I need you to take the fall.

LILY. Oh, no. You can't ask me to do that. I've a baby to live for.

BLACKIE. Your record is spotless. You say that you were on a week long drunk when you stiffed the jeweler and you'll get a measly fifteen months.

LILY. Fifteen months? I won't do fifteen days.

BLACKIE. You won't be spending fifteen minutes behind bars. My lawyers will make a back room deal to get you off completely and the charges dropped. Let's go to the office and you can give yourself up.

LILY. My new friends, the baron and baroness, might be of help.

BLACKIE. You little fool, the gentleman who told you he was a baron goes by another name, Lieutenant Herman Pielmeier of the San Francisco Police Department.

LILY. What about the baroness?

BLACKIE. She's also undercover. That baroness of yours is none other than Lieutenant Hank Abatelli of the Division of Grand Larceny.

LILY. I thought there was something funny about her.

BLACKIE. You've been hoodwinked, my love. Bamboozled. You're an angel for doing this. I'll never forget it.

LILY. I haven't agreed to anything yet.

> (*The* **"BARON"** *and* **"BARONESS"** *return. Though still in costume, they've dropped their false identities. The* **"BARONESS"** *is brandishing a pair of handcuffs.*)

BARON. Are you Lily Dare AKA Mandalay?

LILY. Yes, I am.

BARON. You're charged with the conspiracy and theft of those diamond earrings. Hand 'em over.

LILY. I've never stolen anything in my life.

> (**LILY** *removes the earrings and hands them to* **PIELMEIER.**)

BARONESS. Lady, we've been onto you for months. You've left a trail of hot diamonds from here to Rio.

LILY. Rio?

BARON. Bid tally ho to the high life. You're coming with us.

BLACKIE. This is monstrous! You're railroading an innocent young woman to gain yourselves some free publicity and an ovation at the policeman's ball. Be brave, dear Lily, be brave. This will all be cleared up in a few hours. I'm getting on this right now.

(**BLACKIE** *races out.*)

LILY. Blackie, come back!

BARON/PIELMEIER. Where's your wrap?

LILY. In the dressing room. May I return to my home first?

BARONESS. Sister, it's straight to the county lock up.

(*The "***BARONESS***" fastens the handcuffs on* **LILY.***)*

LILY. Must you put these on me? I promise not to run away.

BARON. We're going to make an example of you. The new San Francisco won't stand for the same filthy corruption of the old Barbary Coast. Those glory days are over.

(**EMMY** *enters holding the swaddled infant in her arms.*)

EMMY. Lily, the darling one refuses to fall asleep without you kissing her good night.

BARON. Get that brat out of here!

EMMY. What's this all about?

LILY. I beg of you. Can't I give my baby a good night's kiss?

BARONESS. You're going places. Into the black Maria* with ya.

(*The two police officers drag* **LILY** *out of the room, as she cries out.*)

LILY. Louise! Louise! Louise!

---

* Pronunciation: Ma-RY-a.

Scene Eight

(1950. **EMMY** *continues her narration.)*

EMMY. Lily waited to hear from Blackie's lawyers. The days turned into months. She was tried and found guilty. Lily spent five years in that state prison. Forsaken by everyone, except you and me, Mick. How rotten that because our careers were on the seamier side, we weren't allowed even one visit. Then came the day we were all waiting for: the day our girl was released from the hoosegow. We were there at the prison gate first thing in the morning to take her home with us.

(1911, the prison gate. **EMMY** *and* **MICKEY** *wait outside.)*

MICKEY. It's good to see that for once in your life you weren't late.

EMMY. And keep the kid sitting in stir for even another minute? How that poor lamb has suffered. I've always likened her to a delicate piece of porcelain. I don't know how she hasn't cracked.

MICKEY. My guess is that someone with Lily's sweet nature manages to stay that way no matter what stones life throws at her.

EMMY. Mick, how do I look?

MICKEY. What does it matter how you look? She hasn't been writing a fashion column for the prison gazette.

EMMY. Well, I didn't wanna be dressed too drab so she'd think I was embarrassed to be seen with her. And if I was too stylish she'd feel lousy she'd been away so long.

MICKEY. Lily's gonna have a lot of new things to be accustomed to. When she got locked up, there weren't any cars on the road.

EMMY. I hadn't even thought of that. There's one thing that's been preying on my mind. What do we tell her about Louise?

MICKEY. I haven't gotten a night's sleep for a week pondering a way to break her the bad news. How could fate have so turned against her?

EMMY. Between you and me, fate deserves a busted lip.

MICKEY. Listen to us. We gotta can the dismals. It's our duty to make Lily thrilled to be back in circulation.

EMMY. You nailed it, conductor. We've been on the wrong track with the moaning and groaning. We'll assume an air of gaiety, as if we're off to a madcap garden party.

MICKEY. That ain't the tone.

EMMY. Well, what is the tone? You got me so muddled. If there's one thing I have a talent for, it's being the mistress of any situation. Now I don't know what's gonna come out of my mouth.

MICKEY. I apologize, Em. What can I say? I love the kid.

EMMY. *(Comforting him.)* I know you do, Mick. I know you do. Here she comes! At least, I think this is her.

> (**LILY** *enters from the prison gate. The five years in prison have completely changed her. She looks drab and dowdy. All of the life has been drained from her.*)

Lily darling! We're here!

MICKEY. Hallelujah! Kingdom come!

EMMY. Let's get a chump's eye view of you. Oh, you look marvelous. Doesn't she, Mick? Rested. You'd never think you were...away.

MICKEY. We're gonna take you home with us now. We've got a room all set up. I'm forever decorating rooms for you.

LILY. *(Tough as nails.)* One stink hole is the same as another. Mick, never con an old con. I know what's waitin' for me freeside. Nothin' but sneers and the brush off. Emmy Lou, is that what they're wearing these days?

EMMY. It's the current vogue. My last husband Phillipe was in ladies apparel.

LILY. I hope it looked better on him. Say, how come you're both here? Shouldn't someone be at home with the baby?

EMMY. Um... That's something we need to talk about.

LILY. Yeah? What gives?

MICKEY. This ain't easy, Lil.

LILY. Mick, is she...dead?

EMMY. No, no. She's in the pink. She really is.

LILY. So? Out with it.

EMMY. You tell her, Mick.

MICKEY. After you were sent up, Emmy Lou and I did our darndest taking care of the baby, but before long the child welfare department came after us.

LILY. Keep goin'.

MICKEY. They were determined to put Louise in an orphan asylum. I grew up in them places. It's something awful.

EMMY. We couldn't let that happen to her. So we went to see Blackie.

LILY. Blackie? That no good, two-timing fuck face.

MICKEY. We figured he owed you one, on account of you taking the rap for him. Well, he heard about a wealthy couple who had no luck having a baby of their own. He managed to convince them to take in Louise.

LILY. Take my baby? And you let him get away with it?

EMMY. It was that or the orphan asylum. *(Near tears.)* Oh, Lily, don't look at us that way. We wanted what was best for the kid.

LILY. You know where she is? You know the name of these people?

MICKEY. Yeah.

LILY. Well, I suppose if she had to be somewhere while I was gone, a fine home is nothing to sneeze at.

EMMY. I knew you'd see it that way. She's a lucky girl to have found these people. He's a doctor. Dr. Robert Carlton.

LILY. They live in San Francisco?

EMMY. Pacific Heights.

LILY. Well, we'd better hurry over.

MICKEY. What for?

LILY. Don't be a dunce. To pick up my baby. She's nearly six years old. In two months, five days and thirteen minutes that is. You got the address on you, Mick?

MICKEY. Stuck in my memory like flypaper.

EMMY. Don't do this, Lily. Let her go. The Carltons will provide her with so much more than you ever can.

LILY. You're talking to the wrong dame if you think I'll let any swells steal my kid. We'll go there right now.

Scene Nine

(The elegant parlor in the home of the Carltons. LILY *and* EMMY *are seated.* MICKEY *stands behind them as they converse with the lovely* MRS. CARLTON *and her husband,* ROBERT.*)*

DR. CARLTON. I must say I hadn't anticipated this. I had been informed the child's mother was dead.

LILY. To the general population, Dr. Carlton, and even to myself, but no more. Tell me about her. Please.

MRS. CARLTON. Mavis is a wonderful child.

LILY. Mavis? Her name is Louise.

MRS. CARLTON. Mavis was my beloved mother's name. Baby Mavis is affectionate and loving. Early on she began to speak. And then to sing.

LILY. She's musical?

DR. CARLTON. Mavis is precocious. She can read and count and even do some addition.

LILY. Her father was good with figures.

EMMY. He was a bookkeeper. Honest to a fault.

MICKEY. A true gent.

LILY. You've obviously done very well by her. I'll be eternally grateful. If you could pack up her little things, we'll take her quickly and be gone.

MRS. CARLTON. Take her? Oh no! Robert!

DR. CARLTON. Miss Dare, you can't be serious.

LILY. Of course I am. She's my child.

MRS. CARLTON. You deserted her for five long years.

LILY. My absence was not my fault.

MRS. CARLTON. Associating with denizens of the underworld was your fault.

EMMY. *(Taking umbrage.)* Now, see here! She was a patsy!

MICKEY. An innocent pawn!

DR. CARLTON. Please. Let us examine this bizarre turn of events with a modicum of hysteria.

LILY. Mrs. Carlton, I suppose I'm naïve. It didn't occur to me that you'd...want to keep her. I am sympathetic. I know what it is to lose a child.

MRS. CARLTON. Is that so? I've lost eleven in childbirth.

DR. CARLTON. Look about you. Mavis has had every advantage. Would you subject her to a life of poverty and privation?

LILY. Dr. Carlton, Mrs. Carlton, for five years my one dream has been to hold my baby in my arms. You have each other. She's all that I have.

DR. CARLTON. For the sake of the child, put aside your own emotions.

LILY. Put aside love? Why, that goes against all human nature.

DR. CARLTON. I am not an ogre, Miss Dare. Can't you see I am fighting for your daughter's future?

LILY. I won't hear anymore. She's mine. Not yours. Where's her bedroom? I'm marching in there and no one can stop me.

MRS. CARLTON. Think of what you're doing. Think of what you're stealing from her.

LILY. Stealing? I gave her the breath of life.

MRS. CARLTON. Giving birth to a child does not make a mother. A mother is one who is there day after day, watching over her every minute to see that she doesn't hurt herself and when she stumbles and scrapes her knee, gives her a butterscotch. A mother is there to see baby's smile and has her handkerchief at the ready to wipe away her child's tears. A mother is one who spanks her when she's naughty and teaches her right from wrong and making plans, choices, decisions. Kissing her and holding her close when she wakes with a nightmare. Nursing her when she has the measles, the mumps, whooping cough, pneumonia, and when she's lying in her bed, with a fever, and the pediatrician says there's no more he can do and you hear her crying,

"Mama! Mama! Why am I so sick? Do something, Mama! Do something!" And you sink to your knees and pray to God to take your life and not hers! That, Miss Dare, is being a mother.

> (DR. CARLTON *puts his arm around his wife.* LILY *is reduced to silence. She sees that she has lost her child.*)

DR. CARLTON. If you still feel you have license to take the child away from a loving home, we will not stop you.

MRS. CARLTON. I can't bear it!

> (MRS. CARLTON *bursts into tears and runs from the room.*)

LILY. I won't take her away. But may I see her one last time? I won't say anything to her.

DR. CARLTON. The nursery is the second door to the left.

> (LILY *exits in the direction of the nursery.*)

You do see that there can be no other way.

EMMY. It's gonna kill her.

MICKEY. At least they get this last farewell. No baby ever loved a mother more.

> (*From the direction of the nursery, we hear the baby's horrifying scream.* LILY *returns.*)

LILY. She wouldn't let me kiss her. I was a stranger.

DR. CARLTON. You must understand...

LILY. You don't have to explain. Dr. Carlton, your family will never see me again.

> (*The three of them head towards the door.* LILY *stops and turns back to* DR. CARLTON.)

Dr. Carlton?

DR. CARLTON. Yes, Miss Dare?

LILY. May I ask one thing? Could you consider changing her name back to Louise? At her tender age, she won't mind. Can you grant me that?

DR. CARLTON. Her name shall be Louise.

> (*Music swells.* LILY *exits, followed by* EMMY *and* MICKEY.)

Scene Ten

(**BLACKIE**'s *penthouse suite.* **LILY** *confronts* **BLACKIE**.)

BLACKIE. Interestingly, we stood in these same places in my penthouse, when last you were at low ebb.

LILY. Please don't ask what I've been doing for the past five years.

BLACKIE. You can be assured of that.

LILY. And don't tell me I'm looking well.

BLACKIE. You can be assured of that.

LILY. *You're* looking well. You're looking splendid. In fact, a trifle overfed.

BLACKIE. I shall promptly speak to my tailor. Lily, I am beholden for the sacrifice you made to save my hide. I pay my debts. My lawyers will draw up an agreement to send you an allowance to be delivered the first of every month.

LILY. What? Five dollars? Ten dollars? You didn't lift a finger to help me when I was locked up for a crime you committed. And I have no doubt you pocketed a good price for selling my baby to the Carltons. You'll pay me back. Oh, you'll pay me back but good.

BLACKIE. Shh. You don't want the butler to hear you being shrill.

LILY. To hell with the butler! Don't you know what I've got on you? The swindles, the crimes, the rackets, the bodies buried. I'm prepared to give it all to the authorities. I have nothing more to lose. There is nothing more you can take from me.

BLACKIE. I have business partners who are not as...even tempered as I. Any threat to their livelihood could result in a warranted act of violence.

LILY. Before you plan knocking me off, perhaps you should listen to my proposal.

BLACKIE. Not a further attempt to turn you into a female Caruso. You must realize you've rather missed the boat on operatic stardom.

LILY. It is true I lacked the proper training to be an opera singer. However, my early years living with my dear Aunt Rosalie did give me the proper training to take on the family business.

BLACKIE. This intrigues me.

LILY. I thought it might. You are going to establish me as the madame of the most exclusive and opulent brothel in San Francisco. Silk furnishings, crystal chandeliers, a velvet sling. Although I regard you as less than slime, I am not unfair. I will give you fifty percent of the business until we recoup your initial investment. After that ten percent.

BLACKIE. I'll take my ten percent. We did well together years ago. We'll do even better now. You're more... seasoned. I suspect we have found our sunken treasure.

LILY. A treasure...

BLACKIE. A penny for your thoughts.

LILY. From now on my thoughts are worth far more than a penny and I may have found my new name. Treasure... Miss Treasure Jones.

ACT II

Scene One

(1950, the cemetery. **MICKEY** *and* **EMMY** *continue reminiscing at* **LILY**'s *grave.)*

MICKEY. Em, you left San Francisco for a couple years.

EMMY. Yeah, I married that rancher in Montana. A religious nut. He insisted on taking his prize heifer with us to church. Thought Big Daisy's soul needed saving. I wasn't around when Lily began her empire.

MICKEY. I was with her the day she found that old wreck of a building. She turned it into the Taj Mahal of cathouses.

EMMY. By the time I stole a horse and escaped from the ranch, Lily was firmly established. I was grateful she took me in. I was no longer a youngster.

MICKEY. We had quite the roster that first year. Gussie. Annabelle. Oh, and that pretty brunette with the funny eye.

EMMY. Winking Wilma. Speaking of young beauties, Louise was growing up fast. Lily kept tabs on her through items in the newspaper and pasted every one of 'em in a red leather scrapbook. The first clipping was the announcement that Miss Louise Carlton was coming out as a society debutante. The clippings kept coming when Louise began her singing career in grand opera.

MICKEY. I'm surprised Lily had the steam to fill those scrapbooks. The First World War kept the place hopping.

EMMY. You ain't kidding. My joints have never been the same. It was a blessing when I was eventually promoted to an executive position.

MICKEY. Lily gave half of every dollar to war charities.

EMMY. Her Aunt Rosalie would never have done that.

MICKEY. She was everything her aunt was...but with a heart.

> (*1916*, **LILY**, *AKA Treasure, appears in a flashback, every inch the madame.*)

LILY. Emmy, I'm laying down the law. As long as this war lasts, we're not giving away any more free liquor. I won't have our dough boys leaving this place stinko. We're here to entertain 'em, support 'em, and we owe it to their mothers to protect their livers.

> (*She waves goodbye to a departing guest.*)

Good to see you, judge. Next time, don't bring candy. Just bring yourself... And tell your chum, Monsignor Ryan, he can put his collar back on.

> (*1950, the cemetery.*)

MICKEY. The years sped by. A blink of the eye and we were in the twenties.

> (*1926.*)

LILY. Mick, I'm gonna need piano men for my new houses in Bakersfield and Junction City. You know the type. Debonair and can play piano with their eyes closed. Say, what day is it?

MICKEY. April twenty-ninth.

LILY. Tomorrow is the thirtieth. Louise is making her concert debut in Chicago. The reviews should be out on Thursday. Didn't we take care of Mr. Wrigley, the fella with the chewing gum factory? He's from Chicago. I'll have him send me them reviews.

> (*Return to 1950.* **MICKEY** *continues with* **EMMY**.)

MICKEY. And they were raves. The Chicago music critics said Louise Carlton was a star on the rise. Within a few years, Louise made her Metropolitan Opera debut as Violetta in *La Traviata.*

> (*Return to 1928.* **LOUISE**, *a lovely young woman, is costumed in Violetta's first act ball gown. She is with her Italian vocal coach,* **MAESTRO GUARDI**.)

LOUISE. Maestro, my revered teacher, here we've arrived at opening night and I sense you're not quite satisfied with my performance.

MAESTRO. *Cara* Luisa, I am not here to plague you the hour of your Metropolitan debut.

LOUISE. I must know before I go out on that stage. I must know where I have failed.

MAESTRO. Your voice...*uno strumento quasi perfetto*[*]. You understand the music in your brain and in your throat. For Violetta that is not enough.

LOUISE. Why must that misguided consumptive prove so elusive?

MAESTRO. The problem, my dear, is that you are too much the gracious lady. Violetta, she is a courtesan, a *cocotte*. A kept woman. She lives by her charms.

LOUISE. Maestro Guardi, I've read everything in the historic records in the original French about the real life lady of the Camellias. I've researched the preponderance of lung disease among the Parisian demimonde.

MAESTRO. Books will not provide the answers you seek. To portray a woman as this requires a boldness of spirit. It takes...how do you Americans say? It takes guts.

> (**LOUISE** *delicately shudders at his vulgarity.*)

LOUISE. Such language, maestro. Can't you say "intestines"?

---

[*] Translation: A nearly perfect instrument.

MAESTRO. *La mia povera piccolo infelice*[*]. This role is a difficult journey for one who has lived a life of stainless purity.

LOUISE. I have conducted myself beyond reproach. I have never given my parents reason for embarrassment or shame.

MAESTRO. How could the doctor and his wife not be proud of such a child?

LOUISE. Yes, they are exceedingly proud of me. You see, I was very much wanted. They were unable to conceive their own child. I was a foundling.

MAESTRO. *Sono senza parole*[**]. In our many hours together, you have never before told me that you were adopted.

LOUISE. I see nothing of consequence to that humble fact.

MAESTRO. Many adopted children spend their lives wondering where they came from.

LOUISE. I have never been the least bit inquisitive. Why should I? It would be foolish to conjecture on the qualities of some hapless girl who may have succumbed to the charms of a wastrel. Who might she be?

(*Gradually becoming lost in reverie.*)

An aristocratic girl...well-schooled...with a gift for music. Blue eyes. Periwinkle blue eyes, ever more beauteous when wet with tears.

(*Pulling herself together.*)

Her passions clearly got the best of her and that is where we differ. In contrast to my more boisterous female colleagues, I shall remain chaste until I wed. Maestro, does that make me less of an artist?

MAESTRO. For some roles? Lucia? Butterfly? No. For Violetta, the music must spring forth from the *pudenda*.

---

[*] Translation: My unhappy little one.

[**] Translation: I am speechless.

(Return to 1950. **MICKEY** *and* **EMMY** *at the cemetery.)*

EMMY. The New York reviews were good but not great.

MICKEY. They said Louise was too refined to be a convincing Violetta. Too genteel.

EMMY. That same year Louise did the "left hand, third finger routine" and married a dyed in the wool Italian aristocrat. The bridal photographs ran in the Chronicle, San Francisco's own Principessa Luisa de Ruspoli de Barragazza.

(1928. **LILY** *reads an account of the wedding in the newspaper.* **BLACKIE** *is counting a thick wad of cash.)*

LILY. The wedding was held in the Basilica of San Marco in Venice. The king of Spain was in attendance.

BLACKIE. I congratulate you on a most successful October. The new houses in Fresno, Stockton, and Calabasas are a raging success.

LILY. Her bridal veil was over thirty feet long and of fifteenth century Alençon lace.

BLACKIE. How rude of me. I couldn't be happier for you and for the child. May I see?

*(***LILY** *hands him the newspaper.)*

LILY. I was wondering when you'd ask. The wedding got two full pages.

BLACKIE. Louise makes a fetching bride. I could use a magnifying glass to identify all of these impressive specimens of international high society.

LILY. You don't need a magnifying glass to see how happy she is. Louise must love the prince very much. And he must be crazy about her. Who wouldn't? Blackie, I wonder if she'll be giving up her singing career.

(1950. **MICKEY** *continues his narration.)*

MICKEY. She didn't. The magazines said Louise Carlton was a modern woman, able to balance both marriage and stardom.

(*Return to 1929.* **LILY** *is with* **EMMY**, *who is carrying a scrapbook.*)

EMMY. Lil, I got a new clipping for you to put in the scrapbook. From Vanity Fair.

LILY. Vanity Fair? What's it say?

EMMY. It's an item how Louise is making...

LILY. (*Gently correcting her.*) She's no longer Louise, Emmy Lou. She's her highness, the principessa.

EMMY. Okay, the principessa will be making her Paris Opera debut next month.

LILY. Do they say what opera?

EMMY. She's taking another stab at Violetta. In New York she nearly got a tomato in the puss.

LILY. And I'm the one person who could help her. Give her the low down on that sort of woman. Well, let's keep track of it. Emmy Lou, *we've* got a debut coming up: a new house in Sausalito. That makes seven. If there's fornication going on in the state of California, you can bet Treasure Jones is making a buck off it.

EMMY. Lady, I gotta run. Wanna pick you up a new scrapbook from the dime store before it closes. This one's so stuffed it's bursting at the seams.

(**EMMY** *exits.*)

LILY. (*With maternal intensity.*) The Paris Opera. *La Traviata.* Louise, do well, my baby, do well.

(*1929, Paris.*)

(**LOUISE**, *again in her Violetta ball gown, is singing "Sempre Libera." She begins singing*

---

* A license to produce *The Confession of Lily Dare* does not include a performance license for any third-party or copyrighted recordings. Licensees should create their own.

in a somewhat stiff lady-like manner and then suddenly something in her clicks, her eyes fairly pop with insightful revelation, and she transforms into a sensual lusty Violetta.)

(Return to 1929, LILY's *bordello in San Francisco.* MICKEY *is at the piano.* LILY *enters.)*

LILY. I see an assortment of characters gathering dust in the parlor.

MICKEY. A lingerie salesman, a testy interior decorator, and a pair of twin sisters from Sacramento. The postman just delivered the mail.

(He hands her a stack of letters.)

Where you been all afternoon?

LILY. A long lunch with my business manager. I tell ya, Mick, bringing that clever little Feltenstein into my empire was the smartest move I ever made.

MICKEY. He asking you to sell off more of your properties?

LILY. That's the ticket. The market is booming and I need the cash to invest. The guy's a genius. Within two months I've tripled my portfolio. The infamous Treasure Jones, a Wall Street tycoon.

(An envelope sparks her interest.)

Here's a letter from that French fella, the kooky artist who stayed with us last winter, Marcel Duchamp.

(She finds an enclosed newspaper clipping.)

What's this? A clipping. He sent me Louise's review in the Paris paper. *"La nuit derniere, la celebre..."*

MICKEY. In English, please.

LILY. "Last night the celebrated American soprano, Louise Carlton, made a spectacular Paris debut." Spectacular, Mick! "She is a Violetta for the ages. She manages to be both the ethereal tragic lady of the Camellias, while exhibiting a decidedly earthy carnality." I hope my baby isn't doing anything dirty.

(1950. **MICKEY** *returns to his narration.)*

MICKEY. Then the day came for Louise's long-awaited San Francisco Opera debut. Once again, the opera was *La Traviata*.

(1930, **LOUISE***'s dressing room at the San Francisco Opera House. She is conferring with the* **MAESTRO** *and is in an agitated state.)*

LOUISE. My nerves! My nerves are in shreds! What if I'm struck mute and no sound emerges from my throat? Tell me it's not scarlet and enflamed. Admit that I'm ruined and will never sing again!

(She opens her mouth. The **MAESTRO** *looks down her throat.)*

MAESTRO. The epithelium and the rima glottidis both appear to be in perfect health.

LOUISE. And yet, Maestro, I'm unable to sing! The music has betrayed me! I can't go on! I can't! I can't!

(Before **LOUISE** *can spiral into complete hysteria, the* **MAESTRO** *slaps her cross the face. She collapses gratefully into his arms, softly weeping.)*

MAESTRO. *(Gently.) La mia povera ragazza spaventata*[*], you have triumphed in Paris, La Scala, Covent Garden. Why should you have a *crise de nerfs*[**] in San Francisco? These are not worldly musical aficionados. They are provincials.

LOUISE. It's as if someone extraordinary is out there. Someone I cannot fail.

MAESTRO. My dear, you are on a never ending quest for perfection.

LOUISE. No. Tonight is different, I tell you. Oh, if Paulo were here. He has the power to calm me when I'm in one of these mad skittish frenzies.

---

[*] Translation: My frightened girl.
[**] Translation: Attack of nerves.

MAESTRO. You have sung many performances of *Traviata*. It is your signature role. You are Violetta.

LOUISE. I made a bungle of the role until one night she came to me. It was as if...as if someone willed me to succeed, and gave me Violetta.

MAESTRO. The performance has been sold out for months. All of San Francisco high society is out front.

> (*An opera box at the San Francisco Opera House.* **LILY** *is present with* **EMMY**. **LILY** *looks every inch the elegant matriarch.*)

LILY. They're all here to see my little girl. I bet there are a dozen millionaires down there in the orchestra and another dozen in the mezzanine.

EMMY. Lil, I've never seen you so radiant. Next to you, those blue blooded society dames look positively anemic.

LILY. What would I do without you, Em? Did you notice the mayor and his wife in the lobby as we walked in? He doesn't dare look me in the eye. He knows I've seen his pecker sticking out of his union suit.

EMMY. I've never sat in a box before. You must have paid a bundle for these tickets.

LILY. Emmy Lou, shortly, the golden curtain will rise and there she'll be: my Louise gracing that stage. I haven't laid eyes on her since she was a toddler. Emmy, where are my opera glasses? Did I forget to bring them? I need to be able to see Louise up close.

EMMY. I got 'em in my evening bag. You gave them to me to hold.

> (*She takes them out of her bag and hands them to* **LILY**.)

LILY. I'm just so excited. Louise singing here at the San Francisco Opera.

> (**LILY** *peers at the stage with her opera glasses. We hear the voice-over whispers of the dowagers around her.* **LILY** *and* **EMMY** *can hear them as well.*)

WOMAN 1. Look over there in the next box. Do you know who that is?

WOMAN 2. No. Who is she? She's quite distingué.

WOMAN 1. It's the bordello madame who goes by the name of Treasure Jones.

WOMAN 2. That's Treasure Jones? She's said to be a woman of the most common sort.

WOMAN 1. The vile trollop shouldn't be allowed in here.

WOMAN 3. Excuse me. I couldn't help but overhear you. Who is that woman?

WOMAN 2. Treasure Jones.

WOMAN 3. The brothel keeper? How dare she show her face in this sacred temple of art?

WOMAN 1. Disgraceful.

WOMAN 2. And at the debut of an elegant opera star and royalty to boot. Louise Carlton is married to an Italian nobleman, you know.

WOMAN 3. How appalling to have her debut sullied. I'm sure the music critics will take note of the presence of Treasure Jones.

LILY. Emmy, let's go.

EMMY. The opera hasn't started yet. You've thought of nothing else for months.

LILY. Let's go, please.

EMMY. Lil, it's your night as well as hers.

LILY. No, it's not. It's all hers. We can't leave through the lobby. There might be newspaper reporters. Photographers. There must be a back exit.

EMMY. Can't you ignore the old biddy hens?

LILY. We should never have come. Someone might connect her name to mine. How could I have been so selfish?

> (**LILY** *rises and begins to leave the box, followed by* **EMMY**.)

WOMAN 1. She's leaving. The harlot.

WOMAN 2. She didn't realize she was at the opera. She thought it was a burlesque show.

> (*The* **WOMEN**'s *laughter builds until it is magnified to the imagined cacophonous sound in* **LILY**'s *head, as she flees the opera box.*)

> (*We return to* **LOUISE**'s *dressing room after the performance. She's with her father,* **DR. CARLTON**.)

DR. CARLTON. Daughter, sixteen curtain calls! Sixteen curtain calls! Louise, the opera house will never recover.

LOUISE. *(Elated.)* Was it sixteen, Papa*? I stopped counting at ten. I was nearly delirious. My poor tenor. His wrist must be aching from my grasp. Tonight it was all there. The music, the drama.

DR. CARLTON. And what an honor for this simple doctor to be the first in the prima donna's dressing room after the performance. There is a crush of admirers clamoring to see you.

LOUISE. Strange. I was told the performance was sold out and yet the box nearest to stage right was empty.

DR. CARLTON. Louise, there could be countless reasons for it to be empty. Otherwise, there wasn't a seat to be had.

LOUISE. My eyes kept returning to that pair of vacant seats throughout the performance. I became rather obsessed with them.

DR. CARLTON. My dear, the performance was a triumph from beginning to end. That is my diagnosis and I stand by it.

LOUISE. Spoken as an eminent doctor.

DR. CARLTON. And as a physician, I can detect the temperature of an audience the same as I can the condition of a...

---

* Pronunciation: pa-PA.

LOUISE. ...Of a gall bladder.

DR. CARLTON. Go on and laugh at me. Oh, if only your mother were here tonight.

LOUISE. My mother? Odd that you say that.

DR. CARLTON. Odd? Your mother may have died two years ago but her love abides with you.

LOUISE. She was a darling. I thought you meant my real mother.

DR. CARLTON. Louise, your mother, my wife, could not have been more devoted.

LOUISE. Papa, of course, she was. But we both know I do have another mother.

DR. CARLTON. Louise...

LOUISE. We've never discussed the woman who gave me birth.

DR. CARLTON. Your adoption was hardly a secret.

LOUISE. In vague allusions, never in detail.

DR. CARLTON. Well, what would you have me tell you?

LOUISE. Who was she?

DR. CARLTON. The adoption was arranged through an intermediary on the condition that the identity of the mother be kept unknown.

LOUISE. Was this upon her request?

DR. CARLTON. Why these questions on the night of your great success in your hometown?

LOUISE. I can't help but be haunted, here in the city where she must have lived; where, perchance, she does live. What dire circumstances forced her to give me up? Papa, I see that I'm unnerving you.

DR. CARLTON. I'm simply at a loss.

LOUISE. Do indulge my morbidity.

DR. CARLTON. You artists are a queer breed.

LOUISE. Triumph often leads to fits of melancholy. Ask the caesars of Rome.

DR. CARLTON. My daughter, you were my princess even before you became one.

LOUISE. I wasn't born a princess. To whom was I born? I must know.

DR. CARLTON. What good could it possibly do you?

LOUISE. How can I be content to bask in my success and the luxury of my life with Paulo, when she could be in need and want?

DR. CARLTON. She might very well be dead.

LOUISE. She's not dead. She lives.

DR. CARLTON. How can you be sure?

LOUISE. Some taut invisible thread connects us. Is she lonely? Starving? Friendless?

DR. CARLTON. Louise, you are becoming overwrought. As your physician, I order you to lie down and close your eyes for a few minutes and then we will bring you to the reception at the Hotel Adagio.

LOUISE. Papa, do you suppose she knows who I am and what I've become?

DR. CARLTON. Louise...

LOUISE. Is she being taken care of? Where is she, Papa? Where is she? Where is she?

Scene Two

(1950. **EMMY** *continues her narration.)*

EMMY. Where was she? Lil was riding high until the stock market crashed. She was wiped out and the men on the breadlines didn't have the dollars to spend on our special brand of entertainment. Lil was down to the original house in San Francisco and lost that in a bank foreclosure. Even Blackie Lambert couldn't bounce back. While I was off with my ninth husband in El Paso, you and Lily picked up a few bucks performing in a gin joint on Larkin Street.

> *(1933, a shabby waterfront bar.* **LILY**, *fragile, worn out and haggard, accompanied by* **MICKEY**, *sings an old sentimental song in the style of "In a Shanty in Old Shanty Town."* After she finishes the song to applause,* **LILY** *goes over to* **MICKEY** *at the piano.)*

LILY. Poker faced ghouls. Singing to them is the same as a French poodle dragging a milk cart. I'm wilting. Hand over my watering can.

> *(**MICK** hands her the purse. She looks inside and finds the flask missing.)*

Say...

MICKEY. I hate seeing you swigging that stuff. Doc Michel says it's poison to your kidneys.

LILY. Aw, quit shaking the tambourine.

MICKEY. Doc Michel says you can't go on downing that liquid tar. It'll kill you.

LILY. Doc Michel! Cheap quack. A house call from him takes you one step closer to a mortuary slab. You gonna give me that flask or not?

---

* A license to produce *The Confession of Lily Dare* does not include a performance license for any third-party or copyrighted music. Licensees should create an original composition or use music in the public domain. For further information, please see Music Use Note on page 3.

MICKEY. I can't.

LILY. Give it to me or I swear I'll sock you one on the snout! I will!

MICKEY. *(Pleading.)* Lil, the boss told me if he caught you boiled again he'd give you the heave-ho. And then I'd have to quit and where will that get us? Singin' "Nearer My God to Thee" for pennies on the street corner.

LILY. Of all the dog and pony joints I've played, this tops them all.

MICKEY. It wasn't easy booking us a spot here.

LILY. *(With alcoholic delusions of grandeur.)* My services as a chanteuse are in demand in the finest gin mills in this city. I'm the Titian-tressed empress of melody.

MICKEY. That was years ago, Lil. Years ago.

LILY. Was it?

> *(Pause.)*

It *was* years ago. Mick, will you forgive me? Forgive me for everything.

MICKEY. No forgiveness necessary.

LILY. Dear friend. I don't know who I am anymore. I've certainly sunk low.

> *(Pulling herself together.)*

Say, remember when we were headlining the Chateau le Noir? Now, that was swank.

MICKEY. Strictly carriage trade.

LILY. Yes, strictly carriage trade. We'd look out from the stage and see the ladies dressed in the latest haute couture. Plumes in their hair.

MICKEY. Plumes in their hair.

LILY. The men with rubies as big as a clam shell in their stick pins.

MICKEY. Big as a clam shell.

LILY. And the food. Remember the champagne suppers after the performance. The caviar. The lobster thermidor. The sweetbreads a la Française.

MICKEY. Ah, the sweetbreads. Lil, what's the point of looking back? Makes the past seem farther away.

LILY. Yes. So far away. You, my pal, have the soul of a philosopher. Now the flask, Socrates, the flask. A couple of snorts and then I promise, I promise, I promise to take it easy.

> (MICKEY *furtively looks around and hands her the flask. She slips it in her purse.*)

MICKEY. Don't let anyone catch you.

LILY. You may kindly inform my public that madama will be holed up in her artist's dressing room. The buzzards.

> (*Lights shift and* LILY *sits at the tiny dressing table with its framed photo of* LOUISE. *She takes the flask out of her purse, turns the photo around so "*LOUISE*" won't look at her and swigs from the flask.* BLACKIE *enters. A derelict, he looks worse off than* LILY.)

BLACKIE. Caught your last number. The rain outside must have rusted your pipes.

LILY. Thanks. You're bad for what ails me.

BLACKIE. Got any cash on you? I need a bottle.

LILY. You can't shake me down, Blackie. Those gin blossoms on your face have turned into roses. You've been on a toot.

BLACKIE. To think that it's come to this. Blackie Lambert begging for scratch from a liquored up tramp.

LILY. Scavenger!

BLACKIE. Let's not argue. We're the oldest of friends. We should be joining forces.

LILY. For what? There's no future for either of us. You're an idiot if you don't realize the money days are over.

BLACKIE. Not for Blackie Lambert. There's life still in me. I can come back bigger than ever. Lil, I'm talking resurrection. And you're going to help me.

> (*He picks up* LOUISE'*s framed photo.*)

LILY. Get your hands off that photo!

(She grabs it back from him and cradles it.)

Louise! My baby.

BLACKIE. It's not right, Lil. It's not right that she's wrapped in chinchilla, an opera star, a princess, while you shrivel away in squalor.

LILY. My silence is all I can offer my child.

BLACKIE. Well, I'm not as soft as you. I'm writing a letter to the Principessa Luisa and telling her everything. If she doesn't agree to the pay-off I'm proposing, I'll let every news hound from coast to coast know who her real mother is: the whorehouse madame, Miss Treasure Jones.

LILY. After all I've been through, you think I'd let you get away with that?

BLACKIE. Lil, it's a daughter's duty. I'm doing this for you as well as for myself. Wait till she gets a load of you.

LILY. Yeah, I look just like the mother of a princess. Her old ma. And you? Look atcha; red faced, saggy jawed, rheumy-eyed, bow-legged, balls hanging to your knees. The great Blackie Lambert. Ha! Ha! Ha!

BLACKIE. Don't laugh at me. Don't ever laugh at me!

LILY. Rummy, find a doorway to sleep it off.

BLACKIE. I'm telling you, the princess is going to pay. She and that royal husband of hers will be singing to a different tune to avoid an ugly international scandal.

LILY. I won't let you do it, Blackie. I won't let you.

BLACKIE. You'll come around. Booze ain't cheap and you're hooked. Look in the mirror. Wino!

LILY. Grave picker!

BLACKIE. You'll do exactly as I say.

LILY. I may crawl in the same gutter as you, but I'm not a beast of prey.

*(**BLACKIE** takes the photo, turns his back on her, and begins to leave.)*

BLACKIE. Lil, I was prepared to give you a prime cut of the deal. I'm in the winner's circle. Bases loaded.

> (*Unseen by* **BLACKIE**, **LILY** *takes a small gun out of her purse.*)

With you or without you, I'll live handsome for the rest of my life.

> (**LILY** *shoots him three times. He stumbles offstage to his death. She returns the gun to her purse and places it in a drawer in the table.* **LILY** *sits down at the dressing table in a numbed state of shock. She remains seated as the scene shifts to her trial for the murder of* **BLACKIE LAMBERT**.)

> (*We hear the voices of the* **PROSECUTOR**, *the court appointed* **DEFENSE ATTORNEY**, *and the* **JUDGE**. **LILY** *listens to them as if in a dream.*)

PROSECUTOR. The prosecutor on behalf of the people of the state of California charges the defendant with murder of the first degree and asks that the penalty be fixed at death.

DEFENSE ATTORNEY. The defense will show that the defendant was not responsible at the time of the crime and that the so-called confession was obtained under duress.

PROSECUTOR. Don't be tricked into sympathy for her. She is a murderess. She broke the law of God and man. She must pay for her crime!

DEFENSE ATTORNEY. Eugene "Blackie" Lambert has a long history of felonies: petty larceny, arson, conspiracy, kidnapping, procuring, embezzlement, forgery, money laundering, perjury, racketeering, extortion, violation of the Mann Act, funeral parlor fraud.

PROSECUTOR. His past does not condone his murder!

DEFENSE ATTORNEY. I tell you it must! My client is but his latest victim. By her silence, she is protecting the object of his latest extortion scheme.

PROSECUTOR. She's a murderess!

DEFENSE ATTORNEY. Who are you protecting? Is it someone you love?

PROSECUTOR. She's a murderess!

DEFENSE ATTORNEY. Is it someone you love? Who?

PROSECUTOR. Murderess!

DEFENSE ATTORNEY. Who?

PROSECUTOR. Murderess!

DEFENSE ATTORNEY. Who?

PROSECUTOR. Murderess!

DEFENSE ATTORNEY. Who?

LILY. Stop it! Stop it! I can't take anymore! How long must I wait? Take my life! The sooner the better! Take it!

JUDGE. It is the judgement and sentence of this court that the defendant, Lily Dare, found guilty of the crime of murder in the first degree, shall suffer the extreme penalty, to be executed and put to death on Friday, the twenty-seventh of January, 1933, between the hours of 10 a.m. and 4 p.m., within the walls of San Quentin Penitentiary by hanging by the neck until you shall be dead, and may God have mercy on your soul.

Scene Three

(A prison cell. LILY, wraith-like, stands in a vacant state of resignation. An Irish PRIEST enters.)

PRIEST. Miss Jones? Miss Dare? What name would you prefer I address you by?

(She doesn't respond.)

You don't seem to care, do you? Despite your violent actions, you are still God's child.

LILY. Child? Did you say "child"?

PRIEST. Yes, even a convicted murderess is God's child. We have ten minutes before we have to escort ye down to tighten the noose around your neck.

LILY. Ten minutes?

PRIEST. Ten minutes it be. As the good Lord's liaison, why, might I ask, did you take this man's life?

LILY. Father, if I should ascend to heaven, God and God alone will know why I fired those shots.

PRIEST. Oh, I'm so forgetful. I'd forget my crucifix if it weren't embedded into me flesh. There is a lady outside who has been begging to see you.

LILY. A lady?

PRIEST. She says she's a dear friend of yours.

LILY. A blonde lady?

PRIEST. As fair as the Magdalene. I'll take that for a "yes" and put an end to her waitin.'

(The PRIEST exits and immediately returns with EMMY, who is attempting to compose herself. LILY stands.)

EMMY. Lily...

PRIEST. I shall leave you ladies be. For the record, you have eight minutes, give or take.

(The PRIEST exits.)

LILY. Have you been out in that cold dank corridor?

EMMY. It didn't matter, as long as there was some hope that I might see you.

LILY. And here we are. Fate has been kind.

EMMY. *(Sobbing.)* No, it's not. It's cruel. Bitterly unfair.

LILY. Emmy, you mustn't cry. There's no time for tears. I hear the execution goes rather quickly.

EMMY. No, no, no!

LILY. The trap door opens, the body falls, and then a clean break of the neck.

EMMY. No, no, no!

LILY. You mustn't weep for me, because I'm not scared. I thought I would be.

EMMY. It's as if you welcomed it.

LILY. I do.

EMMY. You're so brave.

LILY. It takes bravery to live, not to die.

EMMY. How fitting that you should be the one giving *me* courage.

LILY. You've been my friend. You won't forget me?

EMMY. Never. Never.

LILY. You know we're only truly dead when we're forgotten. Now dry your eyes. Where's your handkerchief?

> (**EMMY** *digs in her small bag and finds her handkerchief.* **LILY** *takes it and dabs* **EMMY**'s *eyes.*)

We can't have you walking out of here with your makeup smudged. That wouldn't do at all.

EMMY. *(Tremulously.)* Do I look all right now?

LILY. Ready for a four o'clock with the comptroller. I'm glad that you're the last person from my life that I shall see before...before I go.

EMMY. Lily, there is someone else out in the corridor.

LILY. Mickey?

EMMY. Louise.

LILY. Louise? Here?

EMMY. Oh, and wait till you get a look at her. She really is every inch the princess.

LILY. Have them send her away.

EMMY. Tell her the truth. Tell her who you are.

LILY. Have her know her mother is a murderess? I won't do that to her.

EMMY. Lily, she's waited so many years, the same as you.

LILY. I can't see her. And when I'm gone, you've gotta promise, Emmy, you gotta promise you'll never tell her the truth.

EMMY. What harm will it do then?

LILY. Emmy, swear on everything you hold sacred. Swear on my grave. She must never know! You must do this for me. You must!

EMMY. I promise.

> (**EMMY** *takes her into her arms. The* **PRIEST** *enters.*)

LILY. Is it...time?

> (*The* **PRIEST** *takes a step towards them.*)

EMMY. *(With a blood curdling scream.)* NO!!

PRIEST. You still have a good five minutes. An important personage desires to pay a call on ye. Miss Louise Carlton. At the rectory, we have all of her recordings. Glory be to Saint Padraig, I've had the enormous pleasure of seeing her on the operatic stage. Due to me vow of poverty, regretfully, from a seat in the top gallery, but ohh...

EMMY. *(Beside herself.)* CUT THE CRAP AND LET THE DAME IN!

LILY. Emmy!!

PRIEST. *(Calling outside the cell.)* Miss Carlton?

EMMY. At least you'll be together.

(**LOUISE** *enters. The* **PRIEST** *exits.* **LOUISE** *is surprised to see* **EMMY LOU**.)

LOUISE. I must apologize for invading your privacy. Miss Jones, I am Louise Carlton.

(**EMMY**, *encouraged, chooses to leave them alone. She gives* **LILY** *a wistful smile and before she goes, she blows her friend a farewell kiss. A stalwart little soul,* **EMMY** *exits.*)

I had to see you. The newspapers have all written that when the police opened the door to your hotel room, they discovered a stack of scrapbooks devoted to my career. May I ask why you have shown an interest in me, even before I became a celebrated opera star?

LILY. Oh, I don't know. I suppose I recognized talent. I sing a little myself, you know.

LOUISE. Could this Blackie Lambert have possibly held some knowledge of me that forced you into the role of my protector? And if so why didn't you speak up to save yourself?

LILY. You are a star...royalty. I couldn't have your name dragged into the mire.

LOUISE. What information had he that might have threatened my name?

LILY. Miss Carlton, I am not well.

LOUISE. I was adopted at a very young age. Never told of where I came from. Could you possibly be...?

LILY. I know what you're going to ask. In my current state, I may say something that I vowed I would never reveal.

LOUISE. To whom did you make that vow?

LILY. To someone who had every right to ask for it.

LOUISE. It's true then. You are my mother.

LILY. Miss Carlton, you are quite mistaken. I am not your mother.

LOUISE. Recently, a memory has returned to me. An incident from when I was five or six years old. There was a woman who came into my bedroom. She was gentle and beautiful. I was confused...frightened. She tried to kiss me and I screamed. She went away.

(*A meaningful pause.*)

You?

(**LILY** *looks at her with plaintive eyes.*)

It was you. I see now that your eyes have forever watched over me.

LILY. Oh my. Oh my.

LOUISE. You are ill. Should I call the guard?

LILY. No. It's just my heart. It's so full. Let me look at you. How lovely you are.

LOUISE. If there was something I could do to repay you for your discretion. At any time you could have revealed your identity and brought humiliation upon my head. My mother, a bordello madame. My mother, a murderess. My mother, a cabaret performer.

LILY. You might give me the one thing I've longed for.

LOUISE. And what is that? Do tell me.

LILY. You could give me a daughter's kiss.

(**LOUISE** *lovingly kisses* **LILY**'s *cheek, then kneels and places her head in* **LILY**'s *lap.*)

Everything I've ever suffered has been worth it for this blessing.

LOUISE. Such wisdom of life I could have gleaned from you.

LILY. Child, I give you these words of truth. It's the moments of love that matter. Only the moments of love.

LOUISE. There can be more than a few moments. Everything can be different now. We'll get you a new trial. You'll be set free. My husband and I will take care of you, as you should always have been cared for. Paulo and I have an enchanting palazzo in Venice. It's sunny and warm there. You'll get well. Nothing will be too good for you, my darling.

LILY. If only... If only I could live long enough to see you onstage. What role will you be playing next?

LOUISE. Adriana Lecouvreur in Lisbon.

LILY. Are you pleased with the the mezzo-soprano?

LOUISE. Yes. She is an esteemed colleague. Dame Sybil Porter is an inspired artist and a fabulous Rabelaisian old cunt. You see, Mother, I can say that word now without mortification. Are you familiar with the opera?

LILY. I am. My mind isn't working very well today. I can't recall what happens in the fourth act. Is it a happy ending?

LOUISE. Adriana dies.

LILY. Now I remember. She dies holding a bouquet of Parma violets.

LOUISE. Yes, Parma violets.

LILY. I've never had the privilege of hearing you sing in person. Will you sing for me now? Will you?

LOUISE. If you'd like.

(*About to begin, she stops herself.*)

Mind you, I'm still studying the role. Adriana's act four, scene five aria "Poveri Fiori" is a concert staple of sopranos and surprisingly tricky with its low tessitura and sustained pianissimos. One could cheat and impose more rapid tempi and even transpose upwards, but I'm of the school...

(**LILY** *winces from a pain in her heart and begins to swoon.*)

Mother! Mother! Someone please!

LILY. No! I will not share you with anyone ever again.

LOUISE. Mother!

(**LILY**'s *head falls back. She dies with a beatific smile on her face.*)

Mother! Mother! Don't leave me! Come back! Mother!

(**LOUISE** *sobs into her mother's lap.*)

Epilogue

(1950, the cemetery. **EMMY** *and* **MICKEY** *stand before the elegant tombstone.)*

MICKEY. "Miss Lily Dare. It's the moments of love that matter." I suppose we'll never know who paid for that gravestone.

EMMY. You think it was...?

MICKEY. How could it? How could it?

EMMY. Yeah, how could it?

MICKEY. I suppose we'll never know. And why should we?

EMMY. Oh, look. I hadn't noticed before. Someone left flowers. So pretty. What are they?

(In his heart, **MICKEY** *knows the truth.)*

MICKEY. Violets. Parma violets. *(Thoughtfully.)* Parma violets.

(Emotional music swells.)

End of Play